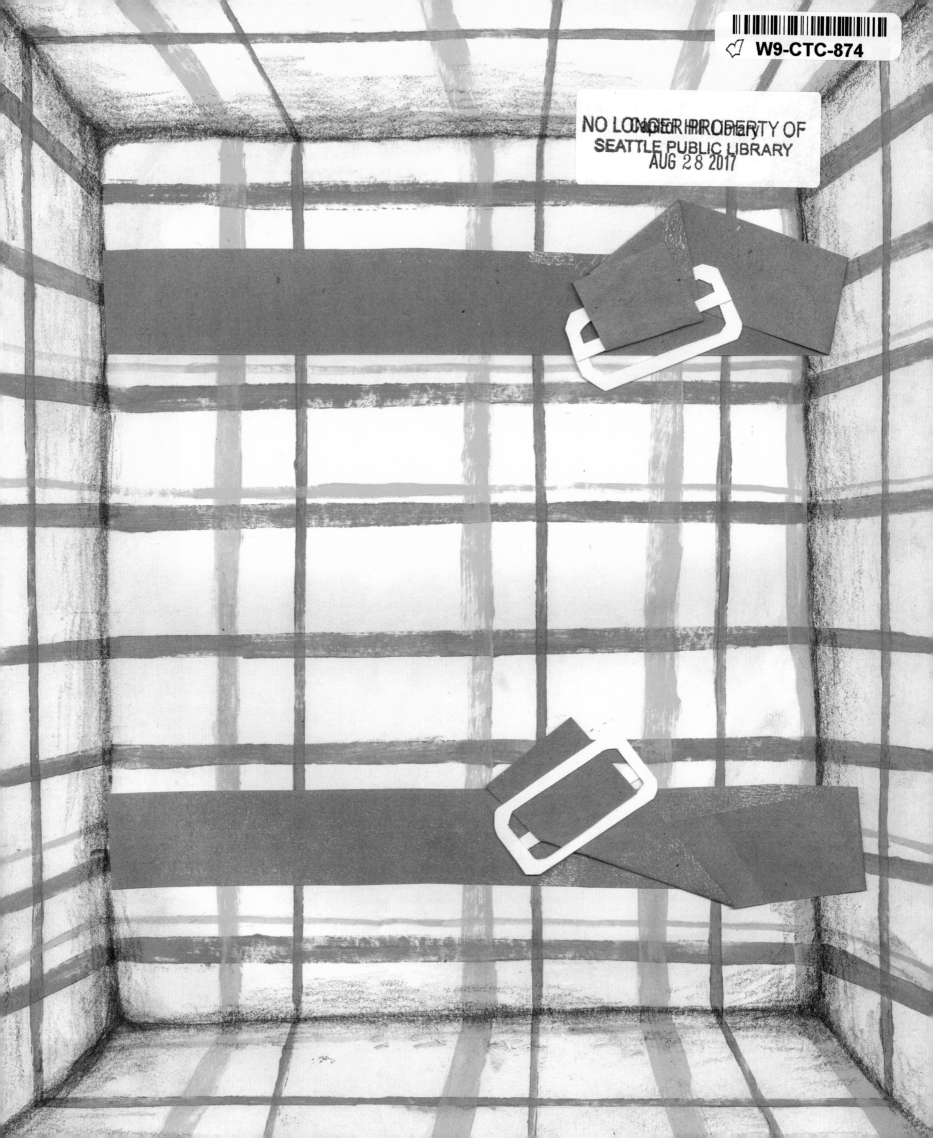

For all those who have to flee their country

I would like to express my deep gratitude to Professor Dieter Jüdt and
Professor Felix Scheinberger for their wonderful advice and encouragement,
to the Walter Benjamin Archive for their expert advice, and to Anne Braune,
Judith Janssen, Jens Kloster, Elfe Marie Opiela, and Clara Weinrich
for their invaluable support and infinite patience. —Pei-Yu Chang

This fictionalized story highlights some of the remarkable aspects of the very real Walter Benjamin, who lived during the tumultuous time of World War II.

It is documented that Mr. Benjamin and his traveling companions successfully crossed the border from occupied France into Spain. It was Walter Benjamin's hope to travel from Spain to the United States. Unfortunately, the Franco government in control of Spain canceled all traveling visas that same day, and the exhausted group was forced to return to occupied France.

Some believe Walter Benjamin, confronted with the possibility of being handed over to Nazi authorities, committed suicide. Others believe he was murdered. However, the next day, his traveling companions were allowed to cross the border. Some believe the guards were touched by the tragic story of Walter's death and allowed his companions passage.

Walter Benjamin's suitcase was never found.

Text and illustrations copyright © 2017 by Pei-Yu Chang
First published in Switzerland in 2017 by NordSüd Verlag AG, CH-8050 Zürich, Switzerland
under the title *Der geheimnisvolle Koffer von Herrn Benjamin*.
English translation copyright © 2017 by NorthSouth Books Inc., New York 10016
Translated by David Henry Wilson

First published in the United States, Great Britain, Canada, Australia, and New Zealand in 2016
by NorthSouth Books Inc., an imprint of NordSüd Verlag AG, CH-8005 Zürich, Switzerland.
Distributed in the United States by NorthSouth Books Inc., New York 10016.

Library of Congress Cataloging-in-Publication Data is available.

ISBN: 978-0-7358-4280-9
Printed in Latvia by Livonia Print, Riga, November 2016.
1 3 5 7 9 • 10 8 6 4 2
www.northsouth.com

Mr. Benjamin's
Suitcase of Secrets

Pei-Yu Chang

Based on a very true story about Walter Benjamin

North South

Not so long ago, a gentleman named Mr. Benjamin lived in a big city. He was a brilliant philosopher and had all sorts of extraordinary ideas. But one day the country in which he lived decided that extraordinary ideas were very dangerous.

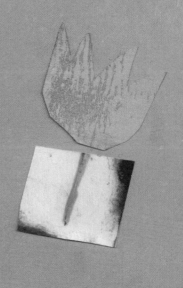

Therefore everyone who had extraordinary ideas had to be arrested.

Every day more and more soldiers came to arrest more and more people. By the time Mr. Benjamin decided to run away, all the streets had been blocked and guarded.

So Mr. Benjamin went to see Mrs. Fittko, who knew all the hidden paths to everywhere.

It was said that she had already taken several people across the border to the neighboring country, where nobody got in trouble for having extraordinary ideas.

When he arrived, there were already a few people with Mrs. Fittko who also wanted to escape. She wanted to help them all.

"We have to pack light," she said. "We can't draw attention to ourselves. We don't want anyone to notice us."

blah blah blah blah blah blah

Soon the day of the great escape arrived!

"Where on earth is Mr. Benjamin? It'll be light soon, and then it'll be too dangerous."

Mrs. Fittko looked nervously around, while the others practiced not drawing attention to themselves.

At last they saw Mr. Benjamin in the distance, huffing and puffing and sweating. In his hand he had a suitcase, and apparently he needed all his strength to carry it.

"Oh, good heavens!" said one of the group.

"Mr. Bennie, you can't be serious!" said another.

They ALL looked at him

AND WONDERED IF Intended to Carry This

across

Now there is one thing you need to know about Mr. Benjamin. Some people thought he was bad luck. Others said he was sometimes just a bit clumsy. But most regarded him as the smartest man they had ever met.

IN ASTONISHMENT

Mr. Benjamin REALLY
← heavy SUITCASE
OVER
THE MOUNTAINS...

And if such a clever man really wanted to take a heavy suitcase across the mountains, then he must certainly have a very good reason for doing so.

And so they all set off—with the suitcase. The road was long. It led them down steep stairs, past blackberry bushes and olive trees.

Then it took them steeply upward over rocks and big boulders.

Once Mrs. Fittko
asked Mr. Benjamin
if it wouldn't
be better for him
to leave his heavy
suitcase behind.

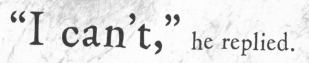

"I can't," he replied.

"The contents of this case
can change everything.

It's the most
important thing to me—

more important
than

my

life."

After countless blackberry bushes, olive trees, and big boulders,
the exhausted group finally reached the border. They only had
to get past the border guards and then they would be free!
The people who were allowed through danced in celebration
of the new life that awaited them. Even Mr. Benjamin could
scarcely hold back his feelings of joy.

But when it came to his turn, he was rejected. "You can't come through. You must go back," the border guard told him.

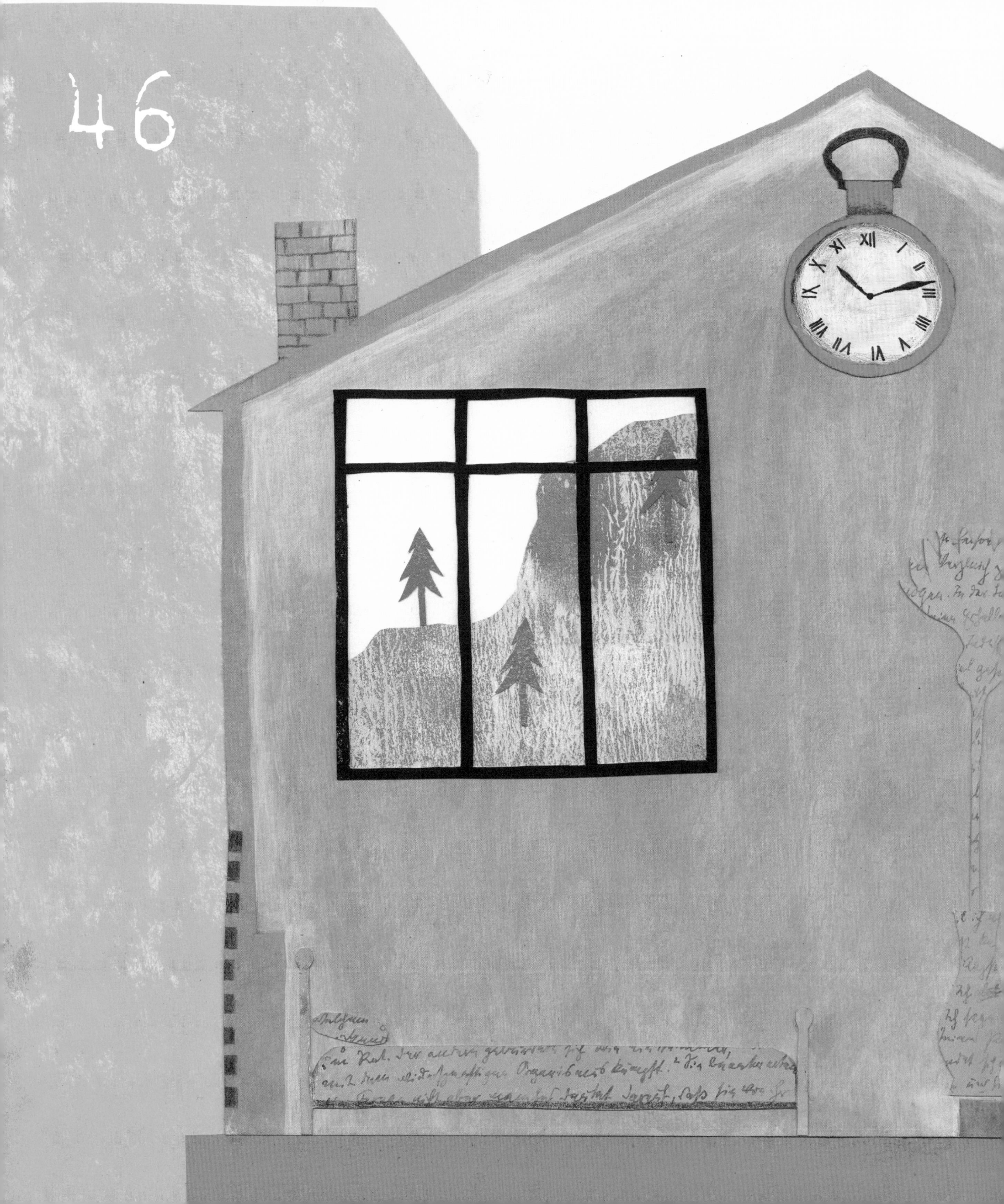

48

50

The last time anyone saw Mr. Benjamin was in a small hotel in the mountains. Then he disappeared— and with him disappeared the suitcase that had been so important to him.

la masi

After his disappearance, the story of the mysterious suitcase spread like wildfire. Many people wanted to know . . .

HAVE

. . . what might have been in it.
What was so important to this
clever man that he wanted to save
it at all costs?

YOU HEARD THE ABOUT  ?

"It must have contained the best philosophical idea of all times," the academics speculated.

"Maybe it was a manuscript about the great history of photography," thought a photographer.

"No, no, my theory is that he wrote a theory in response to *my* theory."

When the generals in Mr. Benjamin's home country heard about the suitcase, they held a summit meeting:

"A collapsible mini-tank."

LEMON & LIME

LEMON & LIME

PEACH & ROSEMARY

SEA BUCKTHORN

Lime

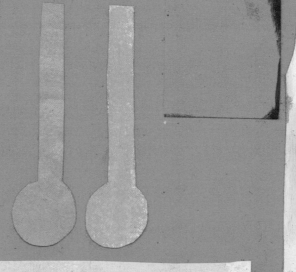

Strawberry

Blackberry

8

green tomatoes

WHAT A LOAD OF NONSENSE

!

The mountain people had a
lively discussion about it over their
cheese and beer.

"It must have contained goodies
he would have missed when he was
so far away."

"Sixty pounds of the best
sausages from his hometown?"

"I reckon it was fifty jars of jam
made by his grandma!"

People went on and on
discussing the mysterious suitcase.

Even today people are still wondering what Mr. Benjamin had in it.

MARKET BOOKSHOP
since 1940

But there is one thing they are all agreed on: it was something very, very extraordinary.

6

MR. BENJAMIN

Walter Benjamin (1892–1940) was one of Germany's most important philosophers and authors, known for having a certain personal charm. A very good friend of his—Theodor W. Adorno—said that he looked like a magician, as he often wore a very tall hat and carried some kind of magic wand.

Walter Benjamin had many interests. He wrote theories about aesthetics and literature, photography, politics, the media, translation, and much more. He also wrote radio plays and invented children's games, did research on color and fantasy, and liked collecting puzzles, children's books, and cards that depicted old Russian toys. Before he fled the country, he left many of his writings with friends or in the public library. That is how a lot of his ideas survived World War II. People from all over the world are still reading about them even today.

MRS. FITTKO

In 1940, an Austrian woman named Lisa Fittko (1909–2005) was locked in a women's prison camp because she fought in the Resistance against Hitler's regime. She managed to escape, and joined the Emergency Rescue Committee—an organization to help refugees. They rescued people who were in danger from the Nazi dictatorship, and generally had to break the law to do so. At the risk of her own life, Lisa Fittko guided the escapees along narrow paths across the Pyrenees as far as the Spanish border. People called it the "F-Route." From there they would make their way by ship to the United States or to South America. For seven months, several times a week, Mrs. Fittko climbed the mountains to a height of over 11,000 feet, until she was forced to leave Europe herself in November 1941. About 80,000 people owed their lives to this secret route.

MS. CHANG

Pei-Yu Chang (b. 1979) studied German language, culture and literature in Taipei (Taiwan) and illustration in Münster (Germany). She loves reading and travel. On a trip to southern Germany in 2015, she heard about the suitcase that had disappeared. She was so fascinated that she simply had to write a story about it. In February 2016, she finished her studies under Professor Felix Scheinberger with *Mr. Benjamin's Suitcase of Secrets*. This is her first children's book.